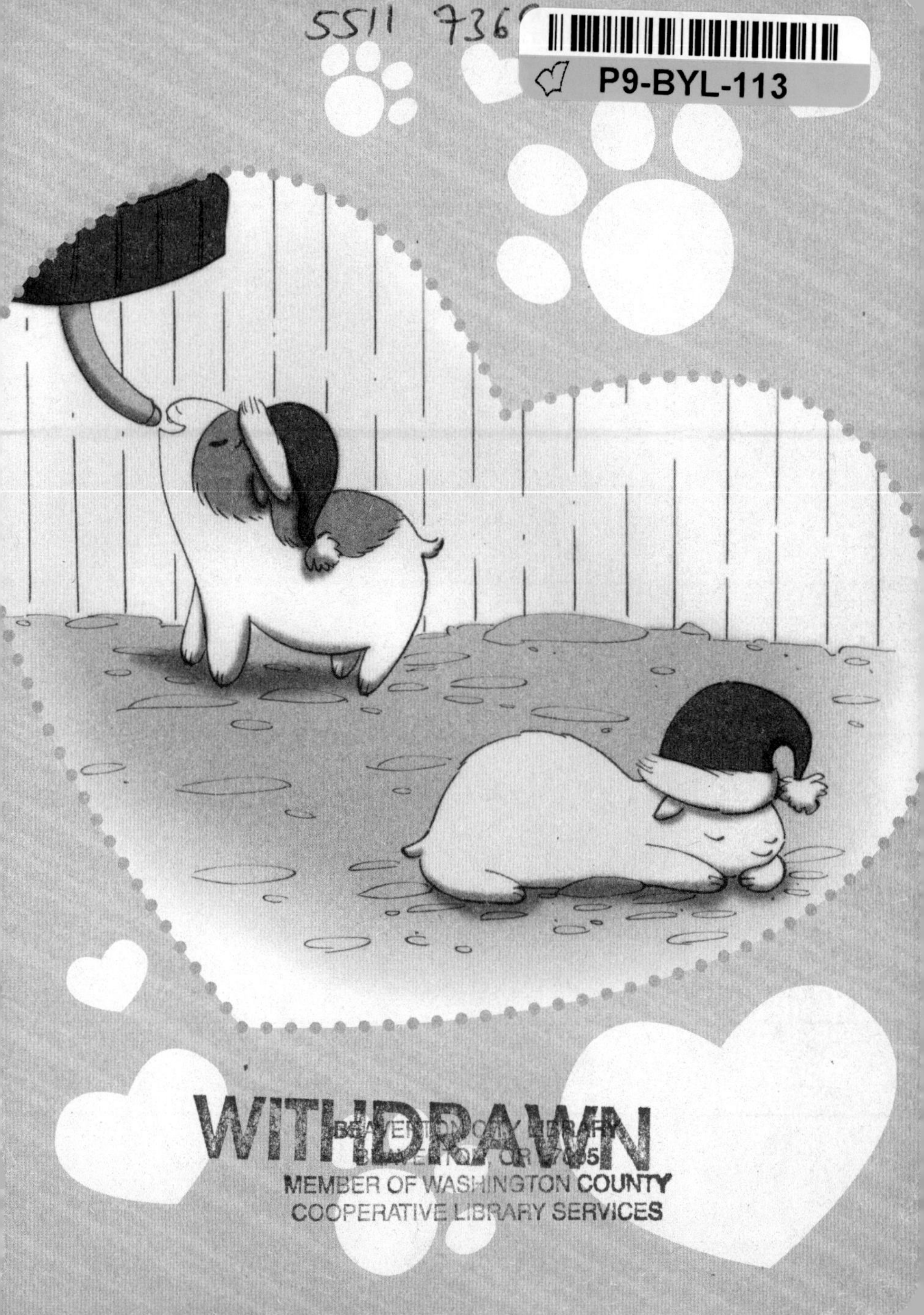

the CRitter club

Amy's Very Merry Christmas

by Callie Barkley ♥ illustrated by Marsha Riti

LITTLE SIMON

New York   London   Toronto   Sydney   New Delhi

LITTLE SIMON

An imprint of Simon & Schuster Children's Publishing Division 1230 Avenue of the Americas, New York, New York 10020 • First Little Simon edition September 2014 • Copyright © 2014 by Simon & Schuster, Inc. All rights reserved, including the right of reproduction in whole or in part in any form. LITTLE SIMON is a registered trademark of Simon & Schuster, Inc., and associated colophon is a trademark of Simon & Schuster, Inc. • For information about special discounts for bulk purchases, please contact Simon & Schuster Special Sales at 1-866-506-1949 or business@simonandschuster.com. • The Simon & Schuster Speakers Bureau can bring authors to your live event. For more information or to book an event contact the Simon & Schuster Speakers Bureau at 1-866-248-3049 or visit our website at www.simonspeakers.com.
Designed by Laura Roode
Manufactured in the United States of America 0814 FFG
10 9 8 7 6 5 4 3 2 1
Library of Congress Cataloging-in-Publication Data
Barkley, Callie. Amy's very merry Christmas / by Callie Barkley ; illustrated by Marsha Riti. — First edition. pages cm. — (The Critter Club ; #9) Summary: As Christmas nears, Amy and her friends in the Critter Club try to find a home for two adorable guinea pigs. [1. Christmas—Fiction. 2. Guinea pigs—Fiction. 3. Animal shelters—Fiction. 4. Pet adoption—Fiction.] I. Riti, Marsha, illustrator. II. Title. PZ7.B250585Aq 2014 [Fic]—dc23 2013042295
ISBN 978-1-4424-9532-6 (hc)
ISBN 978-1-4424-9531-9 (pbk)
ISBN 978-1-4424-9533-3 (eBook)

Table of Contents

Chapter 1

Snowy and Alfie

At her mom's vet clinic, Amy Purvis peeked into the guinea pigs' cage. She had just hung a new toy from its top. *Will they figure out how to play with it?* Amy wondered.

Snowy, the white guinea pig, tried it out first. He sniffed at the jingle bell dangling at the end of a silver velvet ribbon. *Jingle.* The bell rang softly. Snowy darted away and hid inside a tissue box.

His brother, Alfie, came over next. He nudged the bell with his paw. *Jingle-jingle!*

Before long, the two guinea pigs were taking turns batting at the bell.

Amy smiled as she watched them play. "Happy holidays, guys!"

It was a week before Christmas.

Snowy and Alfie had been staying
at the vet clinic for a few days. Their
owner had brought them in because
they seemed sick. They hadn't been
eating or moving around much. But
Amy's mom, Dr. Melanie Purvis,

had known exactly what to do.

"Look at them now!" Amy's mom said, walking up behind Amy. "You see? They just weren't getting enough vitamin C before.

It's a common problem for guinea pigs." Dr. Purvis had fed the guinea pigs lots of oranges and kiwi fruit. "They're just  about well enough to go home."

Amy gave a happy clap. "Yay! Home in time for the holidays!" she said.

Amy loved animals, so she also loved helping out at her mom's clinic. It was in the building right next door to Amy's house, where she lived with her mom. On some weekdays, after school let out, Amy brought her homework over to the clinic. She sat at the front desk, did her reading and math, then helped with chores.

Today she cleaned out cages, refilled water bowls, and took two dogs for walks.

But making the toy for Snowy and Alfie had been the most fun.

"Mom," said Amy. "I just got an idea: I'm going to make a present for each animal at the clinic."

Dr. Purvis gave Amy a hug. "I think that's very nice of you," she said. "Maybe your Critter Club friends would like to help?"

8

"Yes!" said Amy. She and her best friends, Marion, Liz, and Ellie, ran an animal shelter called The Critter Club in their friend Ms. Sullivan's barn. Together, the girls had helped lots of stray animals in Santa Vista find new homes.

Right now, the club didn't have any animal guests. So it was the perfect time for the girls to find some other critters to help.

The animals at the clinic need some holiday cheer, Amy decided. *This is most certainly a job for The Critter Club!*

Chapter 2

Pet Presents

Amy shared her idea with the girls the next day, and they all loved it. After school, the four friends met at The Critter Club. They had some chores to do to keep the barn tidy. Then the rest of the afternoon was free to work on presents for the animals at the vet clinic. And, since it was Friday, they got to have a sleepover at Amy's house that night! Everyone was excited.

"This is going to be so fun!" Ellie exclaimed, sitting down at the worktable.

"I know!" said Liz. "I love making presents. It's one of my favorite things to do around the holidays."

"My mom said we can go over to the clinic whenever we want to deliver them," Amy added.

"It will be fun to watch the animals play with the little things we make!" said Marion.

The girls unpacked the materials they had brought. Ellie's Nana Gloria had lent Ellie her sewing bag. Inside were fabric scraps, colored ribbons, yarn, and buttons. Marion, whose dad did woodworking, had some leftover pieces of wood and sandpaper. Amy had found a few more jingly bells at the bottom of the Christmas ornament box. Liz, the artist, had brought her

art set. It was full of paints, mark-
ers, and a small pad of paper.

"Let's make a list of the animals at the clinic," Marion said. "That way we won't forget anyone."

Amy listed off all the animals while Marion wrote down their names.

16

Next the girls began making gifts. They started simple, with more toys like Snowy and Alfie's jingling bell. Then they decided to use fabric scraps to make the toys extra fun. They made a mouse bell for Mittens the cat, and a cheese bell for Pinky the mouse.

Ms. Sullivan and Rufus, her dog, stopped in to say hello, and the girls excitedly explained their project. Ms. Sullivan smiled. "It sounds like you girls are getting into the holiday spirit," she said.

She helped the girls with
the sewing on a toy fly for a
frog named Croaker.

They even made a floating bell
toy for a fish!

Soon the girls had a special
treat for each of the animals

on their list. They packed up the things they'd made. Ms. Sullivan gave them a ride over to the vet clinic.

"Thank you for all your help, Ms. Sullivan!" Amy called as the girls got out of the car.

Inside, Dr. Purvis was sitting at the front desk.

"Mom, look!" Amy exclaimed. "We have something for every one of your patients!"

Dr. Purvis looked excitedly over their handiwork. "You four have been very busy!" She carefully checked each toy to make sure it was safe for the ani-

mals to play with.

"No loose pieces, no drippy glue they could eat— everything looks wonderful! Thank you so much!"

The girls smiled. "We had fun making them," Liz said. "We hope they have fun playing with them!"

Just then a quiet jingling came

from the far end of the front desk. Alfie was batting at the bell toy in his cage.

Amy brought her friends over so she could introduce them to the guinea pigs. "These are the little guys I was telling you about," Amy

said. Then, remembering something, she looked up at her mom.
"Wait. I thought they were going
home this morning."

Dr. Purvis sighed. "I thought
so too," she said. "But their owner
called . . . with bad news. She just

moved and her new apartment building doesn't allow pets. She's really upset, but she can't keep them."

"Oh no!" Amy cried. Poor Alfie and Snowy!

Christmas was only six days away. It seemed the guinea pigs might not be home for the holidays, after all.

Chapter 3

'Tis Better to Give . . .

"What will happen to Snowy and Alfie?" Ellie moaned. "Where will they go? Who will take care of them? Oh, those poor, poor little guinea pigs!"

The girls were in Amy's room, getting ready for bed. Ellie, Marion, and Liz had unrolled their sleeping bags.

"Ellie, it's okay," Amy said gently. Ellie had a way of getting swept away by her feelings—whether they were feelings of happiness or worry. "My mom will take good care of them for now."

Liz added, "And we can help find them a new home. We are The Critter Club, after all!"

Marion pulled her calendar out of her backpack. "It *would* be nice to find them a new home by Christmas," she said.

Amy nodded. "Maybe we can get them adopted fast!" Amy saw

a folded piece of paper fall out of Marion's calendar. "Hey, what's that?"

Marion picked up the paper and clutched it to her chest. "Oh, nothing," she said with a sly smile. "Just a list of Chanukah gift ideas for my family." Marion paused. "And my *friends*," she added.

"Ooooh!" Ellie cooed. "Let me see?"

Marion shook

her head. "No way! That would ruin the surprise! But I can read *some* of it to you." She unfolded the paper and peeked at it. "I'm doing a number theme this year with my family. Tonight is the sixth night of Chanukah. So I gave my sister, Gabby, six pretty hair clips. For the seventh night, I'm giving my mom and dad seven coupons. They can cash them in for chores I'll do."

Amy, Ellie, and Liz agreed it was a fun idea. "How about the eighth night?" Liz asked.

Marion explained she had the perfect present for Coco, her horse: eight shiny red apples!

Later the girls talked about their favorite things about the holidays. Ellie loved Christmas music. Liz loved the decorations, no matter what holiday they were for. Amy looked forward to having her family together. Marion loved holi-day parties.

"Parties!" Ellie said, putting down her pen. "I love parties too! *We* should have a holiday party!"

"Yeah!" said Liz. "Maybe we could have it at The Critter Club?"

What a great idea! thought Amy.

"We can invite Ms. Sullivan and Rufus," Amy said. "And maybe Snowy and Alfie can come too! Is there anyone else we should invite?"

Then, suddenly, Amy had an idea that surprised her. Usually she liked small parties better than big ones. But at that moment, she thought of a good reason to invite as many people as possible!

"Hey!" Amy exclaimed. "Maybe we can have a party and find a home for the guinea pigs . . . *at the same time!*"

33

Chapter 4

You're Invited

On her way to The Critter Club on Saturday afternoon, Amy stopped her bike at every house she passed. Inside each mailbox, she put a small piece of paper that said:

You are cordially invited to a holiday party
Hosted by Snowy and Alfie
When: Monday, December 21 at 6:30 p.m.
Where: The Critter Club (Marge Sullivan's barn)
Why: Snowy and Alfie need a new home
Come meet them!

By the time she got to The Critter Club, Amy had no invitations left. She had delivered them all, and she'd bet Marion, Liz, and Ellie had done the same with theirs. The girls were meeting at The Critter Club to decorate. They only had two days to get the place ready for the big party!

"Hello Amy dear!" Ms. Sullivan called as Amy walked in. Ms. Sullivan was up on a ladder, hanging lights. Liz was holding the ladder steady.

"Hi Ms. Sullivan!" Amy replied. She knelt down to greet Rufus as he came running over and licked her face. "Hello to you too, Rufus!"

Amy helped out by hanging holly, wreaths, and lights all around the barn. Marion set up folding chairs. Ellie swept the barn floor.

"Ms. Sullivan, thanks for letting us use all these great decorations,"

Marion said as they worked.

"You're welcome!" Ms. Sullivan replied. "I have more holiday stuff than I need. I'm happy you can use it." She climbed down the ladder and dusted her hands off on her skirt. "I have no guests coming this year. So I'm not even sure it's worth the energy to decorate the house."

Amy turned, a wreath in her

hand. "No guests?" she asked. Ms. Sullivan and Rufus lived in a huge house, just the two of them. "Ms. Sullivan, you should come to my house for Christmas! My dad and Julia and Chloe are coming over. It's going to be so fun." Julia was the fiancée of Amy's dad, and Chloe was Julia's daughter. Amy's parents had been divorced for years, but they were still friends.

"No, no!" Ellie chimed in. "Come to *my* house for Christmas. Rufus and Sam could play all day long!" Sam was Ellie's family's golden retriever.

Liz smiled at Ms. Sullivan. "Or you could come to *my* house! My dad is making a tofurkey.

It tastes like turkey, but it's really tofu!"

Marion put her hands on her hips. "And you should come to *mine* for Chanukah! Tomorrow night is the last night!"

Ms. Sullivan laughed and pulled all the girls close to her. "Oh, you girls are so sweet. But you know what? I won't be all alone. I've got Rufus to keep me company. Right, Rufus?"

Rufus ran to Ms. Sullivan's feet. He barked happily in reply.

"See?" Ms. Sullivan said, smiling. "Don't you worry about me. I'll be just fine."

But Amy wasn't so sure. A "just fine" Christmas didn't sound as much fun as a very merry one. She didn't like the idea of Ms. Sullivan and Rufus being all by themselves for the holidays.

And she was determined to do something about it.

Chapter 5

From the Heart

Finally, it was party time. When Amy and her mom got to The Critter Club on Monday evening, Ms. Sullivan, Ellie, Liz, and Marion were already there. The barn looked beautiful. All the lights and the decorations made it look like a holiday wonderland.

"Wow!" said Ellie as Amy and

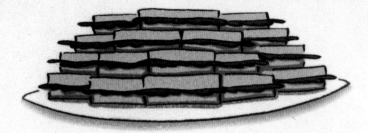

her mom put down a huge tray of sandwiches they had made. "Those should feed everyone!"

"Have you gotten any RSVPs?" Amy asked Ms. Sullivan. "Is anyone coming?"

Ms. Sullivan nodded. "Lots!" she replied. "I think people are *very* excited to meet Snowy and Alfie."

The guinea pigs' cage was on a big table in the middle of the barn. Amy went over to say hello. She noticed right away that they were each wearing a little red-and-green Christmas hat.

"Oh! They're all dressed up!" Amy exclaimed. "How sweet!"

Liz giggled. "It was Marion's idea."

Marion shrugged. "Well, they *are* the party hosts!"

Before the guests started to arrive, Amy and her friends exchanged some small gifts they'd brought for one another. Marion passed out tote bags she had decorated herself. Liz gave hand-lettered bedroom door signs, each with the girl's

name written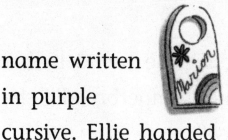
in purple
cursive. Ellie handed
out note cards. "I wrote songs about each of you!" Ellie said proudly. "I can sing them for you later, if you want."

Amy gave her friends homemade treats she had baked the day before. She and her mom loved baking together, especially at holiday time.

Liz sniffed at the bread in her basket. "I smell gingerbread!" she said. "Yummy!"

Walking by, Ms. Sullivan stopped to breathe in the delicious scent. "What a wonderful Christmas aroma!" she said. "When I was a girl, my mother always baked gingerbread cookies at this time of year."

Amy watched Ms. Sullivan's face. Her mouth was smiling, but her eyes looked a little . . . sad. Or was Amy just imagining it?

Amy's friends pulled her in for a big group hug. They thanked one another for their presents. At that moment Amy wished she had brought a present for Ms. Sullivan, too. Was there something they could give her that would help make her Christmas a merry one?

Amy glanced down. Inside their
cage, Snowy and Alfie seemed to be
looking up at the girls.

"Now for Snowy and Alfie's present," Amy said. "Let's see if we can
find them a new home!"

Chapter 6

Fingers Crossed

"It was such a great party!" Liz said as she swung on a playground swing the next day at recess.

"So many people came!" said Ellie, swinging next to her. "The sandwiches were gone before I even got to try one."

"Too bad no one adopted the guinea pigs," Marion added as she batted a tetherball around its pole.

"No one *yet*," said Amy, standing next to the swings. "But remember the older couple that came? They seemed really interested."

Marion nodded. "And also that kindergarten teacher. She was thinking of getting a classroom pet."

Ellie jumped off her swing. "*And* that girl with her mom," she added. "They had all kinds of questions because they've never had pets before."

"Oh yeah," Amy said. "The girl really

wanted to hold the guinea pigs before they left. But her mother was in a hurry to get somewhere. She did say they might come back again today!" Amy crossed her fingers hopefully.

The end-of-recess bell rang. Together, the girls walked toward the school door. "Liz," said Amy, "you and I are on Critter Club duty this afternoon, right?"

Liz nodded. "I think Snowy and Alfie's cage might be due for a cleaning!" She held her nose and laughed.

"You guys must call us if there's any adoption news!" Marion said.

Amy and Liz promised they would.

Chapter 7

Ah-*CHOO*!

After school, Amy left a note for her mom at home.

Then she got on her bike and pedaled down the bike path to Ms. Sullivan's place.

Amy saw Liz's bike leaning against the outside of the barn. Then she noticed two cars in the driveway. One of them looked familiar. *Is that Mom's car? What's she doing here now?* Amy didn't recognize the other car. She parked her bike next to Liz's and hurried inside.

Standing by Snowy and Alfie's cage were the same little girl and mother who had been at the party! Amy's mom and Liz were chatting with them. They all turned as Amy came in.

"Amy, this is Simone," Dr. Purvis said, introducing the girl, who Amy guessed was a little younger than herself. "And this is her mother, Mrs. Cooper. You remember them from the party yesterday?"

Amy smiled and gave a little wave. "Hi!" she said eagerly.

Mrs. Cooper smoothed Simone's long red hair. "Well, we were kind of in a rush yesterday," she said.

"We *had* to come back to visit the guinea pigs again. Simone and I really think they might be good pets for us."

Amy and Liz looked at each other and smiled. "So you're going to adopt them?" Liz asked.

"That's so great!" Amy cried.

"I know!" Simone said, jumping

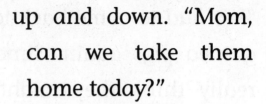

up and down. "Mom, can we take them home today?"

"I *think* we can," Mrs. Cooper said. "I just have a few more questions for Dr. Purvis."

Amy's mom and Mrs. Cooper strolled away to have a chat. Amy and Liz moved to Simone's side. They all looked

down at Snowy and Alfie.

"Have you had a chance to hold them yet?" Amy asked Simone.

Simone shook her head no. "Could I?" she asked eagerly.

"Of course!" Liz said. She opened the cage and gently picked up Snowy. Amy reached in and picked up Alfie. Simone sat down on the barn floor so the girls could put the guinea pigs in her lap.

They crawled on and around Simone as she petted them. Snowy sniffed Simone's shoe. Alfie tried to climb into her pocket. Amy giggled. "They seem to like you already!" Amy said.

Simone beamed. "They do, don't th—ah-CHOO!"

"Bless you!" Amy said.

"Thank you—ah-ah-ah-CHOO!" Simone said, sniffling. "Um, do either of you have a tissue?"

Amy hurried to grab a box of tissues off a shelf. By the time she got back, Simone had sneezed three more times—and was rubbing her eyes. "Ugh. Why are my eyes so itchy all of a sudden?" Simone said.

"All of a sudden?" Amy repeated, feeling a pang of worry. "You don't have a cold or anything?"

Simone shook her head, then sneezed again.

Something was not right here. The sneezing, the itchy eyes. . . . And now Amy noticed a few red blotches on Simone's neck and face.

"Hey, Mom!" Amy called. "And Mrs. Cooper! Come here!"

Dr. Purvis and Mrs. Cooper rushed over. Meanwhile, Simone looked nervously at Amy. "What is it?" Simone said. "What's the matter?"

Amy took a deep breath. "I'm not positive," she said. She looked at her mom. "But I think Simone might be allergic to guinea pigs."

Chapter 8

A Glimmer of Hope

Amy wasn't sure who was more disappointed: Liz and herself, or Simone. She and her mom decided they just couldn't adopt Snowy and Alfie. Simone looked very sad as they left. She sneezed all the way out the door.

Dr. Purvis gave Amy and Liz a quick hug. "Don't worry, girls," she

said. "We will find the right home for them." As she headed for the door, she said, "Oh, by the way, I cleaned the cage this morning. So you don't have to do that." Then she went back to work at the clinic.

Amy and Liz were left alone in

the barn. Amy sighed. "So I guess the guinea pigs just need to be fed," she said. She took the food bowl and Liz took the water bottle.

"Which one of us should call Ellie and Marion?" Liz asked.

"Oh yeah," Amy said glumly.

"They will want to know what happened."

The girls heard a bark and then a voice from the doorway say, "What *did* happen?" It was Ms. Sullivan with Rufus. The dog bounded over and circled Amy and Liz, his tail wagging.

"We were *so close*, Ms. Sullivan," Liz explained.

"Snowy and Alfie almost had a home in time for Christmas. But it didn't work out."

"And tomorrow is Christmas Eve," Amy added sadly.

Ms. Sullivan put an arm around Amy. "Oh well," Ms. Sullivan said. "I'm not really sure guinea pigs celebrate Christmas, anyway."

Amy and Liz couldn't help but laugh.

Then they all watched as Snowy

and Alfie snuggled together in a corner.

"At least they have each other," Ms. Sullivan said quietly.

Amy looked up at Ms. Sullivan's face. She looked a little sad. Her face was scrunched up kind of funny. Ms. Sullivan turned her head away

from Amy. She buried her face in
her arm.

Oh, no, thought Amy. *Is Ms.
Sullivan . . . crying? She does have
the holiday blues!* "Ms. Sullivan,
are you okay?" Amy asked.

"Ah-*CHOO!*"

Ms. Sullivan sneezed loudly into her sleeve. She pulled a tissue out of her sleeve. "Yes, dear," she said, dabbing at her nose. "I'm fine. But I don't love this new pine bedding. Something about it is making me sneeze."

Amy froze. "What new pine bedding?" she asked.

Ms. Sullivan pointed to the wood shavings

lining Snowy and Alfie's cage. "Your mother brought it this morning," she said. "And every time I've come in here today, I've started sneezing!" Ms. Sullivan shrugged. "Maybe we can switch back to the old stuff. Sometimes new is *not* improved, you know!"

PINE
BEDDING

Amy and Liz looked at each other. Smiles spread slow and wide across their faces. Amy could tell they were both thinking the same thing.

"Maybe Simone's *not* allergic to the guinea pigs . . . ," Amy began.

"Maybe she's just allergic to the bedding!" Liz finished.

If they were right, they were going to give one little girl the best Christmas present ever!

89

Snowy and Alfie
Go Home

The look on Simone's face was even happier than Amy had imagined. Simone was holding Snowy in her arms. Right next to her, her mom was holding and petting Alfie.

And Simone wasn't sneezing!

Amy, Marion, Ellie, and Liz stood watching—and smiling—in the front hall of Simone's house. It

was the afternoon of Christmas Eve.

"Wow, I can't believe it was the *bedding* that was making Simone sneeze!" Marion said.

Amy and Liz had told Ellie and Marion everything that happened at The Critter Club the day before.

And Dr. Purvis had called Simone's mom.

"I'm so grateful you girls figured it out!" Mrs. Cooper said.

"Me too!" Simone exclaimed.

Amy laughed. "Well, I'm just happy we turned out to be right," she said. "And Snowy and Alfie look pretty happy about it too."

"By the way, we already changed their

bedding," Liz added, holding up the cage. "This kind is made from paper, so it shouldn't make Simone sneeze."

Liz placed the cage, which the girls had decorated with a big bow, under the Christmas tree. Simone put Snowy inside so she could give each of the girls a hug. "Thank you soooo much!" she cried.

"You've made our Christmas very, *very* merry," Mrs. Cooper added.

"Well, you've made ours merry too," Amy replied.

"Thanks for giving Snowy and Alfie a home," Liz said.

"Happy holidays!" Ellie called as the girls walked out the front door.

Marion added, "Enjoy your first Christmas with your furry family members!"

The next morning, Amy still felt all warm and fuzzy. Maybe it was the brand-new robe and cozy pink slippers from her mom. They *were* super comfy! Maybe it was her cat, Milly, sitting on her lap, or the hot cocoa Julia had made, or the fire in the fireplace.

Maybe it was all of those things—plus being with her family on Christmas morning. It had been a great holiday so far. Amy's dad, Julia, and Chloe had arrived early that morning. They'd had a big, yummy breakfast in front of the fire.

Then they had opened presents. Chloe had made Amy a pretty beaded necklace, which Amy put on right away. Julia and Amy's dad

had given her a stack of
new books they knew
she'd been wanting.
She couldn't wait to

start reading them! And Amy had
loved watching her family open
their presents from her poems for
each one of them.

Of course, Amy's holiday cheer also had to do with Simone and the guinea pigs. She thought about them spending their holiday together, and it made her so happy.

There's only one thing that could make this Christmas even better, Amy thought to herself.

Beep, beep, beep! The oven timer called out from the kitchen. Amy breathed in deeply.

"Do you smell that, Milly?" she said to her cat. "They're ready!"

Amy gently put Milly down on the floor. Then she hurried into the kitchen to check on her top-secret project.

Chapter 10

A Christmas Surprise

"Ready?" Amy whispered to her friends.

Ellie, Liz, and Marion nodded. "Ready!" Ellie whispered, and she reached for the doorbell. The four girls were standing on the front steps of a house on the edge of town.

Ding, dong! They heard the doorbell echoing inside, then a dog barking loudly. The girls giggled.

"She's going to be so surprised!" Liz whispered.

They stood silently, straining to hear. Then came the sound of footsteps getting louder and louder. The door swung open and . . .

"Merry Christmas, Ms. Sullivan!" the girls sang out together.

As Rufus jumped happily around the girls, Ms. Sullivan stood frozen to her spot. She looked completely shocked.

"H-hello!" she stammered. "Merry Christmas to *you*! But . . . now, girls,

107

I told you not to worry about me! Surely you have places to be on Christmas Day!"

Ellie nodded. "Yes, we do," she said. "But we only have one place to be right now, and that's *here*!"

"With you!" added Liz.

"That's right," said Marion. "It

was Amy's idea, but we all agreed. If you weren't coming to us for Christmas—*or* for Chanukah—we were coming to you."

Amy blushed a little bit and shrugged. "Holidays are for spending time with the people you care about," she said. Then she held up a shopping bag. *"And* for gingerbread cookies! Mom and I made them!"

Ms. Sullivan gasped. "Gingerbread? My favorite!"

She smiled, touched that Amy had remembered. "What a lovely idea," Ms. Sullivan said. "Thank you." Then she opened the door wide. "Well, come in, come in. I'll put on the teakettle and get some plates!"

Rufus sniffed the cookies and wagged his tail.

"Oh, Rufus," Amy said, petting him. "Ms. Sullivan, I think we're going to need an extra plate!"

Read on for a sneak peek at
the next Critter Club book:

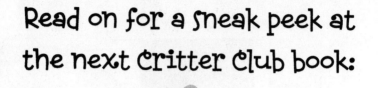

#10

Ellie and the
Good-Luck Pig

Ellie checked her sparkly red watch. "Ms. Sullivan," she said, "what time are they coming again?"

Ms. Sullivan laughed. "Like I said the last time you asked—any minute!"

Ellie sighed. "But that was at least two minutes ago!"

This time, Amy, Liz, and Marion laughed, too. The four girls and Ms. Sullivan were in front of The Critter Club, the animal shelter they ran in Ms. Sullivan's barn. They were waiting to welcome Plum, their newest animal guest.

"Do we have the food ready for her?" Marion asked.

Amy nodded. "My mom says Plum eats all kinds of fruits and vegetables." Amy's mom was veterinarian. She helped out a lot with the animals at The Critter Club. "She also said they are very social animals. We should make sure one of us can come play with her every day."

Liz knelt down to pet Ms. Sullivan's dog. "I wonder what you'll think of Plum, Rufus."

Just then, Rufus started to bark, but not at Liz. He was barking at the road. Everyone looked that way. A pickup truck was just pulling into Ms. Sullivan's driveway.

"She's here! She's here!" Ellie exclaimed. She jumped up and clapped. They'd had all kinds of animals at The Critter Club:

kittens, bunnies, turtles, even frogs. But never an animal like Plum!

The pickup truck came to a stop in front of the barn. A smiling young lady with short dark hair hopped out. "Hi, girls! Hi, Ms. Sullivan!" she said.

"Hi, Anna!" they all replied.

They had met her the day before when she'd come to check out The Critter Club. Ellie felt so happy and proud that Anna had decided it was a good place for Plum—at least for the time being.

Anna walked around to the back

of the pickup. "So are you ready to meet Plum?" she asked.

"Yes!" the girls cried.

Ellie could see the top of a large metal crate in the back of the truck. Anna climbed up and brought it down to the ground.

Inside was the cutest, pinkest little pig Ellie had ever seen!

"Plum!" Ellie squealed. She knelt down beside the crate and peered between the slats. "I'm so excited to meet you!" Plum began to make her own high-pitched pig squeals. She turned around and around in a circle. "And you seem excited to come out!" Ellie added.

"I'm so glad you offered to find a home for her," Anna said as she opened the crate. "Plum has had only our tiny backyard to roam in. She needs more space!"

All of a sudden, Plum rocketed out of the crate. In a flash, she was off. Rufus chased her, barking playfully. The two of them ran around and around the barn. Anna, Ms. Sullivan, and the girls looked on and smiled.

"Yep!" said Ellie. "Space is one

thing we definitely have at The Critter Club!"

The next day, Ellie, Liz, Marion, and Amy sat together at lunch. It was a Monday at Santa Vista Elementary, where the girls were in the same second-grade class.

"Busy weekend, huh?" Ellie said as she unpacked her lunch.

The girls had spent Sunday afternoon playing with Plum. They had also helped Ms. Sullivan start to dig Plum's wallow—a mud hole for her to roll around in. Then Ellie had run off to audition for a play at a local kids' theater.

"How did your audition go?" Liz asked.

Ellie got goose bumps on her arms. "I think it went really well!" she said hopefully. "I tried out for the lead. A lot of other kids did, too. But maybe I have a shot?"

Liz squeezed Ellie's arm. "I bet you'll get it!" she said.

Amy shared some news from her dad, a newspaper editor. "He's going to put an ad in the paper about Plum," Amy said. "Maybe someone will read it and want to adopt her." All the girls agreed that was a great idea.

Liz told her friends about a painting she had worked on over the weekend. "It's going to be a birthday present for my aunt." Liz gasped. "I just remembered! She *loves* pigs! I am totally going to get Plum into the scene somehow!"

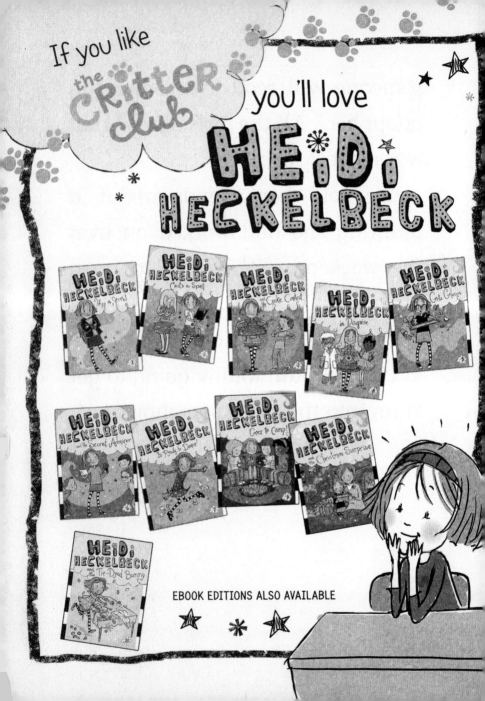